TRIANGLE HISTORIES

THE REVOLUTIONARY WAR

THE BATTLE OF
VALCOUR
BAY

Scott Ingram

BLACKBIRCH®
PRESS

THOMSON

GALE

San Diego • Detroit • New York • San Francisco • Cleveland • New Haven, Conn. • Waterville, Maine • London • Munich

For more information, contact
The Gale Group, Inc.
27500 Drake Rd.
Farmington Hills, MI 48331-3535
Or you can visit our Internet site at http://www.gale.com

Photo credits: cover, pages 5, 7 © North Wind Picture Archives; pages 8, 11 © CORBIS, page 9 © Bridgeman Art Library; pages 10, 18, 28; pages 13, 27 © Mary Evans Picture Library; page 14 © Francis G. Mayer/CORBIS; pages 15, 16, 24 © New York Historical Society, New York, USA/Bridgeman Art Library; page 17 © National Portrait Gallery, Smithsonian Institution/Art Resource; page 22 © National Archives of Canada; page 23 © LCMM Collection; page 26 © Library of Congress; page 30 © Lee Snider/CORBIS

LIBRARY OF CONGRESS CATALOGING-IN-PUBLICATION DATA

Ingram, Scott (William Scott)
  Battle of Valcour Bay / by Scott Ingram.
     p. cm. — (Triangle history of the American Revolution series.
Revolutionary War battles)
Summary: Looks at the strategies employed against the British for control of Lake Champlain that became known as the Battle of Valcour Bay.
Includes bibliographical references and index.
  ISBN 1-56711-778-3 (alk. paper)
  1. Valcour Island, Battle of, N.Y., 1776—Juvenile literature. [1. Valcour Island, Battle of, N.Y., 1776. 2. United States—History—Revolution, 1775-1783—Campaigns.] I. Title. II. Series.

E241.V14I545 2004
973.3'5'0974754—dc21   2003002623

Printed in China
10 9 8 7 6 5 4 3 2 1

CONTENTS

Preface: The American Revolution

Today, more than two centuries after the final shots were fired, the American Revolution remains an inspiring story not only to Americans, but also to people around the world. For many citizens, the well-known battles that occurred between 1775 and 1781—such as Lexington, Trenton, Yorktown, and others— represent the essence of the Revolution. In truth, however, the formation of the United States involved much more than the battles of the Revolutionary War. The creation of our nation occurred over several decades, beginning in 1763, at the end of the French and Indian War, and continuing until 1790, when the last of the original thirteen colonies ratified the Constitution.

More than two hundred years later, it may be difficult to fully appreciate the courage and determination of the people who fought for, and founded, our nation. The decision to declare independence was not made easily—and it was not unanimous. Breaking away from England—the ancestral land of most colonists—was a bold and difficult move. In addition to the emotional hardship of revolt, colonists faced the greatest military and economic power in the world at the time.

The first step on the path to the Revolution was essentially a dispute over money. By 1763 England's treasury had been drained in order to pay for the French and Indian War. British lawmakers, as well as England's new ruler, King George III, felt that the colonies should help to pay for the war's expense and for the cost of housing the British troops who remained in the colonies. Thus began a series of oppressive British tax acts and other laws that angered the colonists and eventually provoked full-scale violence.

The Stamp Act of 1765 was followed by the Townshend Acts in 1767. Gradually, colonists were forced to pay taxes on dozens of everyday goods from playing cards to paint to tea. At the same time, the colonists had no say in the passage of these acts. The more colonists complained that "taxation without representation is tyranny," the more British lawmakers claimed the right to make laws for the colonists "in all cases whatsoever." Soldiers and tax collectors were sent to the colonies to enforce the new laws. In addition, the colonists were forbidden to trade with any country but England.

Each act of Parliament pushed the colonies closer to unifying in opposition to English laws. Boycotts of British goods inspired protests and violence against tax collectors. Merchants who continued to trade with the Crown risked attacks by their colonial neighbors. The rising violence soon led to riots against British troops stationed in the colonies and the organized destruction of British goods. Tossing tea into Boston Harbor was just one destructive act. That event, the Boston Tea Party, led England to pass the so-called Intolerable Acts of 1774. The port of Boston was closed, more British troops were sent to the colonies, and many more legal rights for colonists were suspended.

Finally, there was no turning back. Early on an April morning in 1775, at Lexington Green in Massachusetts, the first shots of the American Revolution were fired. Even after the first battle, the idea of a war against England seemed unimaginable to all but a few radicals. Many colonists held out hope that a compromise could be reached. Except for the Battle of Bunker Hill and some minor battles at sea, the war ceased for much of 1775. During this time, delegates to the Continental Congress struggled to reach a consensus about the next step.

During those uncertain months, the Revolution was fought, not on a military battlefield, but on the battlefield of public opinion. Ardent rebels—especially Samuel Adams and Thomas Paine—worked tirelessly to keep the spirit of revolution alive. They stoked the fires of revolt by writing letters and pamphlets, speaking at public gatherings, organizing boycotts, and devising other forms of protest. It was their brave efforts that kept others focused on liberty and freedom until July 4, 1776. On that day, Thomas Jefferson's Declaration of Independence left no doubt about the intentions of the colonies. As John Adams wrote afterward, the "revolution began in hearts and minds not on battlefield."

As unifying as Jefferson's words were, the United States did not become a nation the moment the Declaration of Independence claimed the right of all people to "life, liberty, and the pursuit of happiness." Before, during, and after the war, Americans who spoke of their "country" still generally meant whatever colony was their home. Some colonies even had their own navies during the war, and a few sent their own representatives to Europe to seek aid for their colony alone while delegates from the Continental Congress were doing the same job for the whole United States. Real national unity did not begin to take hold until the inauguration of George Washington in 1789, and did not fully bloom until the dawn of the nineteenth century.

The Minuteman statue stands in Concord, Massachusetts.

The story of the American Revolution has been told for more than two centuries and may well be told for centuries to come. It is a tribute to the men and women who came together during this unique era that, to this day, people the world over find inspiration in the story of the Revolution. In the words of the Declaration of Independence, these great Americans risked "their lives, their fortunes, and their sacred honor" for freedom.

Introduction:
"Her Rigging Shot Away"

★ ★ ★ ★ ★

In early October 1776, the British navy was about to take total control of Lake Champlain. The 120-mile-long, 12-mile-wide lake that separated New York and the New Hampshire Grants—the area known today as Vermont—was a key passage from north to south. The only section of the huge body of water not under British control was in the southwest. In that area, a small American fleet was anchored in Valcour Bay, a narrow channel between the New York shore and tiny Valcour Island. The British were confident that Valcour Bay too would soon fall under their control.

The American resistance to the British warships could hardly be called a navy. It was barely even a fleet. Fifteen boats of various sizes had been outfitted with cannons and swivel guns, small cannons that could fire in any direction. The commander of the fleet was Benedict Arnold, a general in the Continental army.

Even with his vessels armed and ready, Arnold knew that his fleet would be no match for the British warships sailing south down Lake Champlain. The British battle group consisted of about thirty warships, manned by experienced crews, and it had twice as many cannons as the American ships.

To make up for his disadvantage, Arnold had chosen a location that he could defend without an exchange of side-to-side cannon fire, called broadsides, which the smaller American ships could not withstand. Valcour Bay was so narrow and rocky that only two large British ships would be able to sail into it at once. Arnold assembled his smaller vessels in a curve across the channel from Valcour Island to the mainland. By positioning the ships from end to end, the Americans could fire broadsides at the British ships. The British, however, could return fire only from their forward, or front, guns.

On October 11, scouts informed Arnold that the British fleet was on the opposite side of Valcour Island, in the main body of the lake. Arnold hoped to lure the British into the channel. He did not foresee victory. His goal was simply to delay the British long enough to prevent them from taking control of the entire lake.

Benedict Arnold miscalculated the strength of British firepower.

As part of his strategy, Arnold sent his biggest ship, the *Royal Savage*, out to engage the British warships. After an exchange of fire, the *Royal Savage* was supposed to turn back to the channel and lead the British into a trap. Arnold, however, overlooked one key factor: The large British guns gave them an enormous firepower advantage. As soon as the *Royal Savage* sailed into range of the British ships *Inflexible*, *Maria*, and *Thunderer*, the roar of cannon broadsides echoed across the white-capped water.

From his position on his ship *Congress*, Arnold saw the devastating effect of the British guns on the *Royal Savage*. "One of her masts was wounded and her rigging shot away," Arnold later reported.

With a broken mast and tattered sails, the *Royal Savage* drifted helplessly, raked by cannon fire and grapeshot pellets. Within minutes, it had run aground on Valcour Island. With the largest American ship already out of service, the Battle of Valcour Bay began disastrously for the patriots.

From Hope to Despair

★ ★ ★ ★ ★

The fall of 1776 was one of the darkest periods of the American Revolution for the colonial patriots. The conflict between Great Britain and the colonies, begun in April 1775, had been under way for almost eighteen months. By October 1776, the American forces were totally outnumbered, outgunned, and in retreat.

Many patriots had been hopeful after early battles at Fort Ticonderoga and Bunker Hill in the spring of 1775 had shown that colonial fighters could stand their ground against more-experienced British soldiers. The fact that the patriots had driven a large British force out of Boston by early 1776 had led many colonists to believe that independence would be achieved quickly.

The early patriot success, however, only resulted in British leaders turning the full weight of their military might toward

After an overwhelming show of force by the patriots in the early months of the American Revolution, British troops evacuated Boston by ship.

America. By the spring of 1776, the Royal Navy of Great Britain had set up a blockade of the entire Atlantic coast to prevent goods and troops from moving freely between the colonies. A force of more than thirty thousand redcoats, as British soldiers were known, had landed on Staten Island in New York Harbor. A force nearly half as large had landed in Canada and was headed south to join the British in New York.

Against these odds stood the commander of the Continental army, George Washington, and those colonists who refused to give up their dream of a free nation. One man who was deeply committed to the cause of independence was a wealthy Connecticut merchant named Benedict Arnold. Arnold, in fact, had been one of the first men to offer his services in the cause of independence.

Immediately after the Battles of Lexington and Concord in April 1775, Arnold had marched the Connecticut militia unit he commanded to the Boston area, where he was commissioned as a colonel. Arnold requested permission to lead his unit in an

9

The American attack on Fort Ticonderoga, led by Colonels Ethan Allen and Benedict Arnold, completely surprised the British.

attack on Fort Ticonderoga, a British fort located on the southern end of Lake Champlain in northeastern New York.

In early May 1775, Arnold's unit joined forces with the so-called Green Mountain Boys led by Ethan Allen. On May 10, the Americans under Allen and Arnold surprised the British and captured Fort Ticonderoga, a stronghold that housed more than fifty large cannons. Those big guns were eventually hauled to Boston and set up in a ring around the British in the city.

A month later, on June 17, 1775, the Americans and British fought a bloody battle on Bunker Hill, outside of Boston. Although that battle ended in a British victory, the British suffered terrible losses and withdrew from their conquered ground to Boston. The Americans had proven that they could hold their own on a battlefield against skilled British troops.

As a result of this early success, Washington and his command decided to launch a military campaign against the British in Canada. The commanders knew that they had men who were good fighters, but they needed time to transform the American army into a solid fighting force before it engaged in large-scale battles. An attack on Canada, they hoped, would distract the British from the American colonies and give the Americans time to turn independent militia units into a disciplined army.

10

Arnold, who had returned to Washington's headquarters in Cambridge, near Boston, after the victory at Fort Ticonderoga, had won the general's respect with his bravery and determination. When the decision was made to invade Canada, Washington named Arnold to lead an attack against one of Canada's largest cities, Quebec City.

In mid-September 1775, Arnold led a force of about one thousand men north across the Maine wilderness to attack Quebec City. At the same time that Arnold left Cambridge, a patriot force under Colonel Richard Montgomery left Fort Ticonderoga and moved north to attack Montreal, another large city in Canada. The mission to Canada became one of the greatest failures of the Revolution, and, in many ways, it marked the beginning of the dark days that Americans faced in the early years of the struggle.

Arnold's campaign was doomed from the start because the maps he had of the northern Maine wilderness were inaccurate. The maps were intended to be misleading. The colonists who remained loyal to the king, called Tories or Loyalists, had drawn and printed them that way to trick the patriots. Arnold's map showed a distance of 180 miles across Maine to Canada; in truth, it was more than 400 miles.

As a result of the deception, the American troops became hopelessly lost, and several officers insisted on returning to Boston with their men and supplies. The Americans who remained were forced to eat tree bark, their dogs, and even their shoes to survive. To add to the

Colonel Richard Montgomery led a successful attack on Montreal, Canada.

11

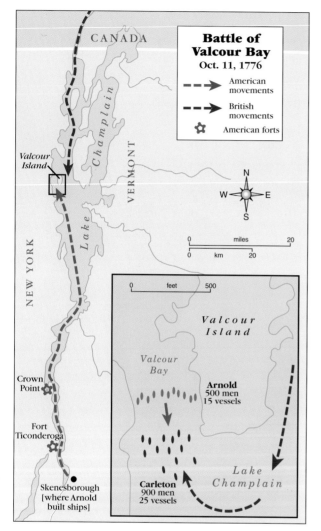

CANADA

VERMONT

Champlain

Lake

Valcour
Island

NEW YORK

N
W   E
S

0   miles   20
0   km   20

0   feet   500

*Valcour
Island*

*Valcour
Bay*

Arnold
500 men
15 vessels

*Lake
Champlain*

Crown
Point

Fort
Ticonderoga

Carleton
900 men
25 vessels

Skenesborough
[where Arnold
built ships]

misery, weather conditions became brutally cold because the force had left so late in the year, and the journey dragged on into November.

Despite the obstacles, a determined Arnold and his small force slogged for more than two months through rain, mud, and snow toward Canada. When the force stumbled out of the dense forests across the St. Lawrence River from Quebec City in mid-November, Arnold had fewer than six hundred half-starved troops to attack the British stronghold.

Several days later, Montgomery successfully occupied Montreal, west of Quebec City. The royal governor of Canada, General Guy Carleton, was forced to flee to Quebec City with his troops. After setting up fortifications in Montreal, Montgomery took as many troops as he could spare and set off to assist Arnold.

Unfortunately for the Americans, icy rain began to fall, and a large number of Arnold's troops became ill. The attack on Quebec City was delayed, and the brutal Canadian winter set in. The Americans' problems then became even worse. Following the usual military procedure of the time, Arnold wrote out a battle plan to inform the commanding officers in the colonies of his strategy. He had given the letter to an Indian scout to deliver to the Americans in Fort Ticonderoga. From there, the plan was supposed to be carried back to Washington's headquarters.

It so happened that the Indian scout was actually a British spy, and instead of carrying the letter to Fort Ticonderoga, he delivered it to Carleton. The British immediately began to reinforce the defensive positions around Quebec City, where Carleton now knew the Americans planned to attack.

When Montgomery arrived at Arnold's encampment in December with a force of 350 men, he and Arnold agreed on the final plans for their attack. They knew that it had to take place before January 1, 1776, when the six-month enlistment period for the majority of their troops ended. Few men were likely to reenlist to serve in the bitter cold of the Canadian winter. Their best chance for success, Montgomery and Arnold decided, was a surprise night attack.

General Guy Carleton, the royal governor of Canada, escaped to Quebec City in a small fishing boat.

The Battle of Valcour Bay

This painting depicts the death of Colonel Montgomery in the first moments of battle in Quebec City.

On December 31 at 2:00 A.M., the Americans launched an attack from two different positions outside Quebec City. The plan was to pinch the British defenders between the two sides and destroy them. The temperature was below zero, and a howling blizzard had reduced visibility to a few feet. The British, who had been alerted to the Americans' plans weeks earlier, were ready. In the initial action, Montgomery was killed and Arnold was seriously wounded in the leg. The attack was a complete disaster for the patriots. More than sixty Americans were killed, and about three hundred were taken prisoner by Carleton's forces, which lost only five men.

Arnold spent the winter of 1776 in Montreal while he recovered from his wound. In the meantime, the British navy was setting up its blockade along the Atlantic coast and bringing

14

huge forces to New York. Another British force landed in Quebec and marched to Montreal to drive out the Americans.

By June 1776, Arnold and his men were marching south from Montreal. He was the last American to leave Canada when he boarded a boat at the northern end of Lake Champlain. Like those of many patriots, Arnold's initial hopes for independence had given way to doubts about whether the British Empire could be defeated.

The ill-fated American attack on Quebec, shown in this illustration on a handkerchief, led Arnold to question if the Americans could defeat the British.

British Strategy

General William Howe planned to blockade New England.

The British forces that arrived in New York in the spring of 1776 were under the command of General William Howe, the commanding officer of troops at Bunker Hill a year earlier. Howe understood the Americans' weaknesses, and he had developed a strategy to bring a quick end to the war. He wanted to cut off New England, the center of the rebellion, from the middle and southern colonies, where anti-British feelings were not as strong.

To accomplish this, Howe first planned to gain control of the lower Hudson River at New York City, which was a Loyalist stronghold. From there, he intended to move north up the Hudson River and march overland to link with Carleton's forces. By the fall of 1776, according to Howe's timetable, the force from Canada would have control of Lake Champlain. The Hudson River–Lake Champlain line, together with the ocean blockade, would encircle New England and choke off that region from the rest of the colonies.

For his part, Washington suspected that Howe would attempt to control New York City, and he had marched most of his army to the region to defend it. Although few American military leaders understood the extent of Howe's plan, Arnold knew all about it. During Arnold's retreat from Montreal, spies in Carleton's camp had passed the information to him.

Unfortunately for the Americans, Arnold was far from the main patriot force in June 1776. There was no way he could alert the patriots gathered in New York City and ask for reinforcements to be sent north to interrent Carleton's force as it moved south. Even if there had been, there was little that Washington could have done. His twenty-thousand-man army was already badly outnumbered by Howe's force, and he could not spare anyone from New York City to go north.

Rather than sending news of the plan ahead to Washington, Arnold continued to row south down Lake Champlain. He hoped to link up with the small American force stationed at Crown Point, a fort on the southwest shore of the lake near the waterway that connects it with Lake George. After he rowed almost one hundred miles to the American fort, Arnold and his small force arrived on July 7, 1776, three days after the Continental Congress had approved the Declaration of Independence.

Arnold's news of Howe's plan caused alarm among the patriot force at Crown Point, commanded by General Horatio Gates. Their concern was increased when Arnold bluntly told his comrades that the Americans had no chance at defeating the large, well-armed British force under Carleton. Their only hope, he believed, was to delay Carleton so that he could not link up with Howe before the winter set in.

General Horatio Gates commanded the patriot forces at Crown Point.

The American commanders understood that, if the two British forces were to meet before then, British warships would sail south from Canada. Because of its 120-mile-long, north-south direction, Lake Champlain was an ideal highway to Lake George and then to the Hudson River. If British ships reached the Hudson River before the lakes froze, they would be able to tighten the noose on the American army and the New England colonies. Patriot soldiers and civilians would be forced to endure a bitter winter without food or other supplies. There was little doubt that such a result would crush the American Revolution.

Gates, Arnold, and other officers knew that their fight to prevent the British from joining forces would be fought on water. There were no roads in the thick forests between Canada

17

General Guy Carleton (1724–1808)

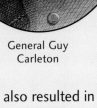

General Guy
Carleton

For the first two years that Benedict Arnold served in the Revolution, his chief opponent was General Guy Carleton, an Irishman who was a career officer in the British military. Arnold, who was by nature a bold and sometimes reckless commander, considered Carleton a weak leader. Carleton, however, was very popular with both the British and French colonists of Canada.

Carleton first came to Canada in 1754 to serve in the French and Indian War, which gave control of previously French Canada to Great Britain. He became the governor of Quebec in 1768 and immediately made efforts to improve relations with the French Canadians. Carleton's efforts resulted in the passage of the Quebec Act by the British Parliament in 1774. This act granted the French Canadians freedom of religion and representation in the Canadian government.

The passage of the Quebec Act hardened many American colonists' attitudes against their own royal governors who refused to secure rights for them, as Carleton had for those under his control. Carleton's sponsorship of the act also resulted in great loyalty to him from the French Canadians. This, in turn, kept them from joining the American attacks on Montreal and Quebec City.

In 1782, Carleton became the last British commander of troops in America. It was his task to surrender New York City to Washington. He resumed his governorship of Quebec in 1784, and took on the task of helping Loyalists from the American colonies start new lives in Canada.

and lower New York that would allow a large army to march south. Arnold and his fellow commanders assumed that the British would send large warships ahead of their troop transport ships to establish safe passage. Once the passage was secured, troops would be ferried south to attack Crown Point and Fort Ticonderoga. British control of those locations would permit more warships to be brought south from Canada.

As formidable as the British naval forces were, Arnold knew that they would encounter natural obstacles. Lake Champlain narrowed and grew shallower at the southern end. Having owned several large merchant ships of his own before the Revolution, Arnold was aware that the large British warships would have difficulty maneuvering in the tight quarters of the southern lake. Thus, it made sense, he believed, to engage the advance force at the point where the lake narrowed.

At that time, however, America had no naval vessels on the lake and no battle-tested crews or gunners to fight. With no time to lose, Arnold requested that a fleet of twenty small gunboats, called gondolas, be built. He knew these boats would be outgunned by the bigger British ships, but he was confident that he could use them to outmaneuver and harass Carleton into a delay.

The First American Fleet

Arnold's request for constructing a fleet was approved by Washington, who also gave Arnold full command of the operation. Soon, shipbuilders, sail makers (called riggers), and workers from across New England arrived in Skenesborough, New York, a village at the southern end of the lake known today as Whitehall.

As the Americans did throughout the war, Arnold faced supply problems right away. Trees for lumber to build the fleet had to be cut miles away and hauled to the construction site. In addition, there was not enough iron for nails. Food, guns, and

★

On July 4, 1776, Samuel Adams added his signature to the Declaration of Independence.

★

powder were also in short supply. Most importantly, there were few men in the area with any naval or battle experience to recruit for crews. Arnold was forced to draft three hundred men from militia stationed at Crown Point. Throughout July and August, while carpenters, sail makers, and laborers built small gunboats, Arnold assembled several hundred "wretched, motley" sailors to man the vessels.

Despite the obstacles, the Americans had enough time to build the fleet because the British also faced difficulties. There was no direct water route from the St. Lawrence River in Canada to the Richelieu River, which flowed into the northern end of Lake Champlain. This meant that the huge British warships that had sailed from Great Britain had to be disassembled and hauled overland, then reassembled. That time-consuming task kept the British busy for much of the summer.

By early September 1776, an American fleet had been assembled at Skenesborough. This first fleet of the American navy consisted of fifteen ships, with à total of seventy cannons, manned by about five hundred sailors and gunners. Arnold's command ship was the *Congress*, which had eight cannons and ten swivel guns. The swivel guns were capable of firing grapeshot in any direction, like giant shotguns.

By late September, the newly built boats were ready for battle. Several larger ships had also been added to the fleet. These were captured British merchant vessels that had been outfitted with cannons. Of the captured ships, the *Royal Savage*, with twenty-two guns, was the largest fighting ship.

The fleet sailed north in search of a position that would give it an advantage in a battle against its more powerful foe. On September 23, Arnold found an ideal spot in the rocky half-mile-wide channel between Valcour Island and the western shoreline, south of Plattsburgh, New York. The two-mile-long, one-mile-wide island shielded the fleet from ships in the main

★

In August 1776, British forces led by General William Howe defeated George Washington's army in the Battle of Long Island.

★

20

The Battle of Valcour Bay

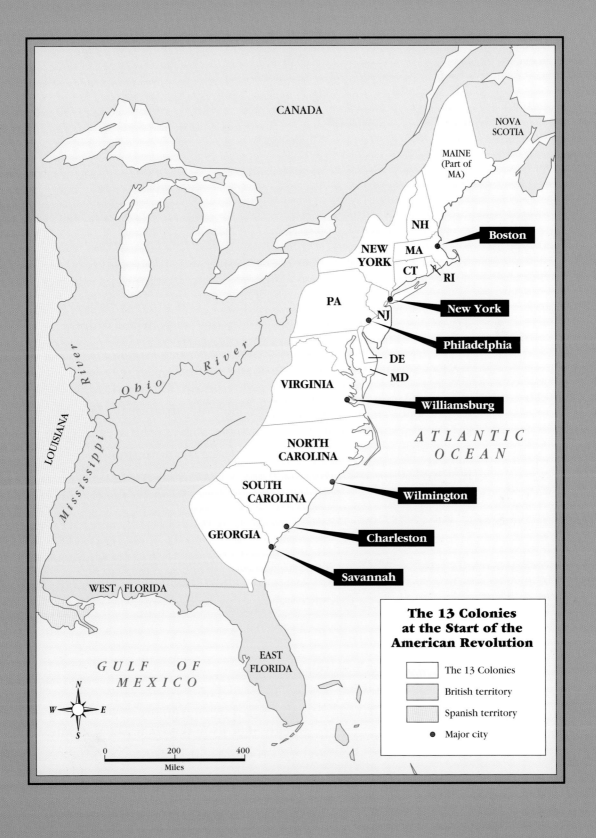

CANADA

NOVA SCOTIA

MAINE
(Part of MA)

NH

NEW YORK

MA

CT

RI

Boston

PA

NJ

New York

Philadelphia

DE

MD

VIRGINIA

Williamsburg

*ATLANTIC
OCEAN*

NORTH
CAROLINA

SOUTH
CAROLINA

Wilmington

GEORGIA

Charleston

Savannah

LOUISIANA

Mississippi River

Ohio River

WEST FLORIDA

EAST
FLORIDA

*GULF OF
MEXICO*

N
W E
S

The 13 Colonies
at the Start of the
American Revolution

☐ The 13 Colonies

▨ British territory

▨ Spanish territory

● Major city

0   200   400
Miles

body of the lake. The rocky channel at what was known as
Valcour Bay was too narrow for large ships to navigate. To
take advantage of the tight quarters, Arnold planned to set his
boats bow to stern across the channel. This arrangement would
allow them to fire broadsides, while the large British ships
would have to use front or rear cannons.

On October 4, a British force of twenty-nine ships and seven
hundred men under Carleton and Admiral Thomas Pringle set
sail from the northern end of the lake in search of the American
ships, which they had learned of from spies in the area. It was
the first wave of a planned British force of more than six
hundred ships and nine thousand soldiers that were to close
the link in Howe's strategic chain around New England.

The experienced British sailors, used to battles on the ocean,
soon realized that lake warfare was different. In some places,
the water was so shallow that the cannons had to be removed
from the warships and transported individually on smaller vessels
to deeper waters so that the big ships would not bottom out.

"A Very Hot Fire"

The British fleet's search for the American ships ended on the
morning of October 11, 1776. In fact, it was the Americans
who first spotted the British ships east of Valcour Island.
Arnold and his officers quickly met to make final plans. Some
of Arnold's staff believed that they would be trapped in their

The Gunboats of Valcour Bay

To build a fleet for lake warfare, Arnold knew he needed vessels that were fast and maneuverable. Eight of the new boats constructed for his tiny fleet were gondolas, or small, flat-bottom gunboats. The standard gondola was about fifty-four feet long and fifteen feet wide with a single mast. The mast had two sails, but its main power came from twenty large oars called sweeps. The boat required a crew of forty-five men, most of whom were assigned to the sweeps.

For weapons, a typical gondola carried two nine-pound cannons (the poundage indicated the weight of the cannonball it fired), one on each side. The largest cannon, a twelve-pounder, was mounted in the bow. In addition, each gondola had several swivel guns. The swivel guns fired grapeshot, iron pellets that could shred enemy sails or drive off enemy boarding parties. Perhaps the most amazing aspect of the gondolas was that, even with a full crew, cannons, shot, and powder, their draft—the depth they sat in the water—was only two feet. As streamlined as gondolas were, though, life on them was uncomfortable and dangerous. The boats had open decks, and the crew slept in the open air surrounded by supplies and weaponry.

Gondolas, such as the one pictured in this modern-day reenactment, maneuvered effectively for lake warfare.

narrow channel and pleaded with Arnold to fight in the open water. Arnold refused. He wanted the enemy to come to him.

At about 11:00 A.M., they did. Arnold sent his largest ship, the *Royal Savage*, out to initiate the action. Within minutes, the American ship was riddled with holes and its sails were destroyed. The crew ran the warship aground on Valcour Island and fled into the woods. Shortly thereafter, a party from the British ship *Loyal Convert* landed on the island, boarded the *Royal Savage*, and turned its guns on the American ships. The Americans had to fire on their own ship to keep it from firing back at them.

Soon, the thunderous blasts of cannons and shrieks of splintering wood echoed across the lake. By 11:30 A.M., several smaller British gunships had managed to get within one hundred yards of the line of the American fleet. Arnold later wrote, "At half past 11 the engagement became General, & very warm. . . . The Enemies Ships . . . [came] within musket Shott of us. They, Continued a Very hot fire with Round & Grape Shott."

Arnold's ship, the *Congress*, took many direct hits, but the Americans also returned fire, with deadly results. The *Carleton*, named in honor of the British commander and governor, lost half its crew to American cannon fire. As the battle continued through the afternoon, however, the superior British firepower took a terrible toll on the Americans. Arnold described some of the damage to his ships in a report:

American and British naval forces bombarded each other in the battle on Lake Champlain. Both sides sustained heavy damage.

Arnold's Court-Martial

Today, Benedict Arnold's name is a synonym for "traitor." Before Arnold betrayed the American cause, however, he was considered one of the patriots' bravest and most determined officers. Even so, he was always arrogant, and he was often at odds with other officers, who resented his snobbish behavior. This attitude caused problems for Arnold even before he went over to the British side.

At the time, military officers often used their own money to buy supplies for their units, with the assurance that they would be repaid by the government. Arnold, who had become wealthy through trade in the Caribbean, paid the expenses for his troops who attacked Fort Ticonderoga in 1775. On his return to Cambridge, Arnold submitted a bill for his expenses to the Continental Congress that was highly inflated. (In other words, he added more money to the bill, hoping to make a financial profit from his victory.)

Arnold left to lead a force to Canada before the bill was settled, and he became enraged when his account was challenged. During the winter of 1776, while he recuperated in Montreal from his wounds, Arnold seized British supplies stored there. Some of the food and weapons were given to his troops. The rest Arnold kept for his own personal use, as well as to sell. He considered it payment for his previous expenses.

When he returned to New York in July 1776, Arnold was accused by another officer of using military supplies for personal profit. Arnold denied the charge, and the controversy resulted in a court-martial trial in the summer of 1776. Arnold was furious at the challenge to his command and insulted every officer in the court. General Horatio Gates, who desperately needed Arnold to supervise the construction of the fleet to be used in Valcour Bay, stepped in and asked the court to clear Arnold of the charges.

The court agreed. Arnold was soon supervising construction and recruiting crewmen, but his bitterness over the dispute lingered. Arnold's belief that he was not properly respected or rewarded by the patriots was a major cause of his eventual treason.

This map shows the positions and courses taken by the American and British naval forces in the Battle of Valcour Bay.

The Congress & Washington … sufferd greatly. … The New York lost all her officers except her captain. [T]he Philadelphia … Sank. … We suffered much for want [loss] of Seamen & Gunners, I was obliged myself to Point Most of the Guns on board the Congress, [which] received Seven Shott between Wind & Water, was hulled [hit on the side by cannon-balls] a dozen times, had her Main Mast Wounded in Two places & her Yard in One.

Although the damage to the American vessels was substantial, it was clear to the patriot officers and sailors that Arnold's decision to position the fleet in Valcour Bay had prevented total defeat. Hampered by the narrow channel and the direction of the wind, the British commanders were unable to bring their biggest ships into the bay. At about 5:00 P.M., the early autumn light began to fade, and the British ships dropped anchor at the southern end of Valcour Bay.

Despite the weak condition of the American fleet, Carleton and Pringle did not want to risk a nighttime battle in the narrow channel. They decided to wait for dawn to finish off their enemy.

Under Enemy Guns

Soon after nightfall, Arnold and his commanders met aboard the Congress. All agreed that the damage to the boats and the loss of men meant that the fleet could not fight another day. The damaged ships would have to slip past the British fleet and make their way south to Crown Point.

American and British gunboats fought at close quarters in the narrow channel.

Arnold came up with a risky plan to secretly row the gondolas and the larger ships past the British fleet in the dark. He ordered the crews to muffle their oars with canvas so that they would not squeak in the oarlocks. They were to row close to the shore of Valcour Island with their lanterns unlit. Then, once in the open lake, they would make their way as quickly as possible to Crown Point.

Somehow, Arnold's plan worked. Some historians say the plan was a success because the British were busy tending to their wounded men. Others claim that the roar of flames and exploding powder supplies on the *Royal Savage* distracted the British lookouts. No matter how the escape was accomplished, it was a shock to the highly confident British. It also increased their respect for Arnold, for both his choice of a defensive position and his escape. Carleton later wrote,

> We . . . Anchored . . . opposite the Rebels . . . expecting in
> the morning to be able to engage them with our whole
> fleet, but, to our great mortification [horror] we perceived
> at day break, that they had found means to escape us
> unobserved. . . . Thus an opportunity . . . was lost, first by
> an impossibility of bringing all our vessels to action, and

The Battle of Valcour Bay

afterwards by the great diligence used by the enemy in getting away from us.

By dawn, the Americans had reached Schuyler's Island, about nine miles south of Valcour Island. In the early morning light, Arnold saw that several vessels were not seaworthy enough to continue. He ordered the damaged boats to be sunk so that the British could not repair them for later use. The remaining fleet proceeded south. Few of the ships had enough undamaged rigging to set sails, so the crews were forced to row the boats into a stiff wind.

Meanwhile, the British had discovered the Americans' escape and set off after Arnold's fleet. They overtook the first American ships just north of a landmark known as Split Rock that jutted into the lake from the western shore. Throughout that day, October 12, what Carleton described as a "running battle" took place, with the Americans trying to row their ships out of range of the fast-sailing British warships. Two of the largest American ships, the *Washington* and the *Jersey*, surrendered after taking numerous British broadsides.

As darkness fell, Arnold realized that his fleet would not be able to outrun the British. His men could not last another day at the oars. Rather than surrender, however, Arnold ordered all

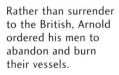

Rather than surrender to the British, Arnold ordered his men to abandon and burn their vessels.

the American vessels to be run aground and set on fire. On October 13, the Americans destroyed their fleet in a bay on the eastern shore of the lake that was known as Ferris' Bay (today called Arnold's Bay). This was the final action of the encounter that became known as the Battle of Valcour Bay.

Epilogue

Arnold left his burning ships and led his exhausted force south to Crown Point, where they arrived on October 14. Gates, who greeted the men as they entered the fortifications, described the events in a letter: "Few Men ever met with so many hair Breadth [e]scapes in so short a space of time…upwards of 200 with their Officers escaped with Genl Arnold."

With Arnold's exhausted men in need of care and the large British force bearing down on Crown Point, Gates believed that Fort Ticonderoga, on higher ground farther south, would offer more protection. Once Arnold and his men ate and rested, the entire force was moved to Ticonderoga.

When Carleton's ships soon sailed within sight of Crown Point, they found it abandoned. He ordered his ships to continue south to Ticonderoga, but strong winds from the south prevented them from making way. Carleton was stranded at Crown Point for more than a week while he waited for a change in the wind.

During that critical time, thousands of patriot militia reinforcements arrived at Ticonderoga. By the time Carleton arrived, it was late October, and more than twelve thousand Americans had assembled to repel the redcoats. Carleton knew that his siege of the American fort could last months, and he had received word that ice was forming on the northern end of the lake. He did not want to expose his troops to winter conditions. Carleton had also learned that Howe's troops had defeated Washington in New York, and he was confident that his men could do the same to the Americans at Fort Ticonderoga in the

★
In October 1776, George Washington's army was defeated by British forces in the Battle of White Plains.
★

Carleton's decision not to attack Fort Ticonderoga (pictured above) gave the Americans time to rebuild their confidence and determination.

spring of 1777. He decided to turn his fleet back and head to winter quarters in Montreal.

That was one of the most crucial decisions of the Revolution. In those winter months, the Americans achieved two badly needed victories at Trenton and Princeton in New Jersey. When the British returned to Ticonderoga in the spring, they faced a more confident and optimistic foe.

The Battle of Valcour Bay was the first naval battle between the Americans and the British. It resulted in a loss for the patriots, but that loss won them valuable time. Naval historian Admiral Thomas Mahan wrote of the battle, "The little American Navy was wiped out, but never had any force, big or small, lived to better purpose or died more gloriously."

The Battle of Valcour Bay

Glossary

blockade to isolate an enemy by means of troops or ships
broadsides firing all of the cannons on one side of a warship at once
channel a waterway between two areas of land
court-martial a military trial of a soldier or officer
deception trickery or dishonesty
fleet a large group of war or transport ships
fortification something constructed for defense
Loyalists American colonists who remained loyal to England, also called Tories
mast a long, vertical pole above the deck of a sailing ship that supports sails
militia a fighting force made up of regular citizens
patriots soldiers who fought against the British in the American Revolution
redcoats a nickname given to British soldiers because of their red uniform jackets
rigging the cables, ropes, and sails of a ship
strategy a plan of action

For More Information

Books

Fritz, Jean. *Traitor: The Case of Benedict Arnold.* New York: Paper Star, 1997.
King, David. *Benedict Arnold and the American Revolution.* San Diego, CA: Blackbirch Press, 1998.
Smith, Carter. *The Revolutionary War: A Sourcebook on Colonial America.* Brookfield, CT: Millbrook Press, 1991.

Websites

The American Revolution
www.theamericanrevolution.org
This website features information about the entire war and has good biographies.

The Battle of Lake Champlain
http://odur.let.rug.nl/~usa/E/champlain/champxx.htm
This essay is a good source about the Battle of Valcour Bay, which was also known as the Battle of Lake Champlain.

Index